A WEREWOLF
NAMED OLIVER JAMES

WITHDRAWN

Nicholas John Frith

ARTHUR A. LEVINE BOOKS
AN IMPRINT OF SCHOLASTIC INC.

A NOTE ON WEREWOLVES:

The myth of the werewolf has been around for many centuries and crosses many cultures. The werewolf is a shape-shifter who transforms from a human into a wolflike creature. There are said to be many ways to become a werewolf.

One of these is to be born one, transforming under the influence of a full moon.

ISBN 978-1-338-25433-4
10 9 8 7 6 5 4 3 2 1   18 19 20 21 22
Printed in Malaysia   108
This edition first printing, July 2018

For anyone who ever missed a bus

Oliver's mom always told him to come straight home after band practice. Dinner was at six o'clock sharp.

As usual, he waited for
the bus with his friends.

But, this evening, something odd happened.

All his friends ran off
before the bus arrived.

"How strange," thought
Oliver James.

And when the bus did turn up . . .

. . . it didn't stop!

"How will I get home now?" sighed Oliver James.

Eventually, a man came up to the bus stop.
"Excuse me, mister," said Oliver,
"do you know what time
the next bus comes?"

But the man just shouted,
"HELP! A WEREWOLF!"
and ran away.

"A werewolf?"
said Oliver James.
"Where?"

But how had that happened?

It was just so . . .

Suddenly, Oliver James could run
SUPER-FAST.

He could leap **SUPER-HIGH.**

GAS

He was
SUPER-STRONG.

Oliver James howled
with excitement.

OWWWW-OWOOOOO!!!

He couldn't wait to go to
school tomorrow, to tell
all his friends about this.

But, look! He wouldn't even have to wait that long! There was his friend Sam coming round the corner.

"Hey, Sam!" shouted Oliver. "You'll never guess what!"

But Sam just shouted,

"HELP! A WEREWOLF!" and ran away.

"Don't be scared!" cried Oliver. "It's only me!"

PECKNOLD'S

Just then, the clock on
the corner struck six.
Oliver had forgotten
all about the time.

"Oh, no!" he said.
"Dinner's at six o'clock sharp.
I'm going to be late!"

Oliver James raced home at
SUPERNATURAL SPEED.

Seconds later, he skidded to a halt
outside his house. He was home . . .

. . . but could he really go in?
"What if my parents are
frightened of me, too?"

But he was late for dinner,
and his mom would be cross.
So he took a deep breath —

— and went inside.

And what an **AMAZING** surprise! His mom and dad weren't frightened of him at all.

"How was band practice?" said Dad.
"Dinner's ready," said Mom.
"You must be hungry."
"I am," said Oliver James.

And he was still **SUPER-HUNGRY** in the morning, too.

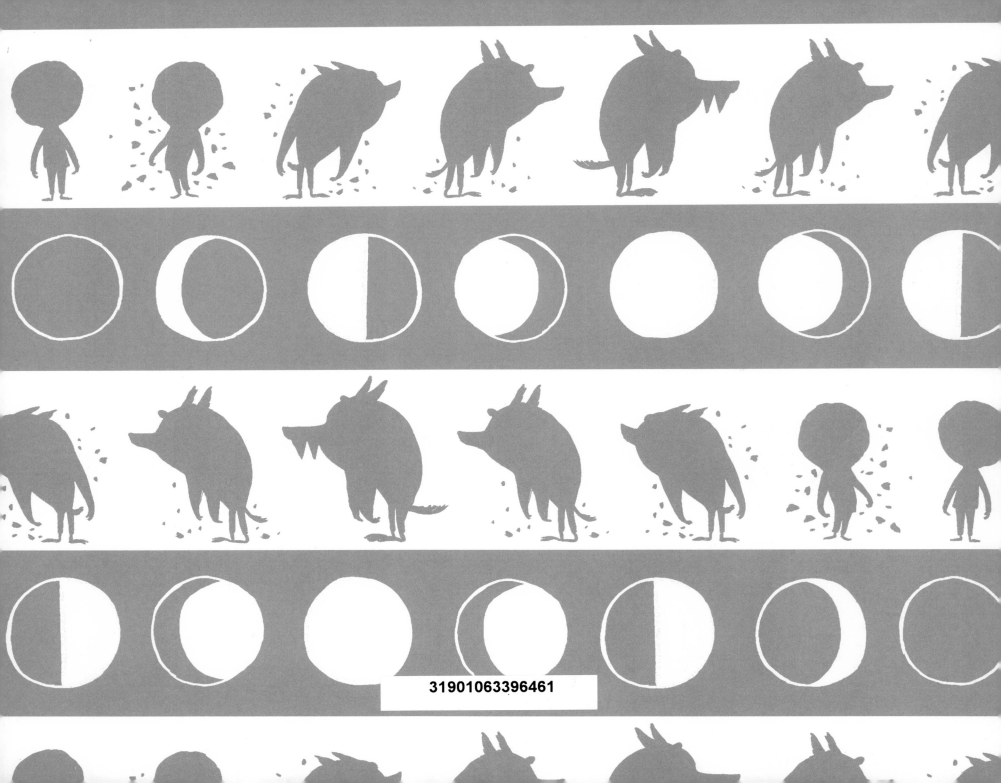